Produced by Kroha Associates, Inc.
Middletown, Connecticut.

Printed in the United States of America.

ISBN 1-56326-114-6

Grown-ups Have More Fun?

One spring afternoon, Minnie and her friends were walking home from school. Birds were singing, flowers were blooming, and the air was soft and warm.

"It's such a pretty day," Minnie said. "I wish I hadn't spent it in school!"

"Me, too!" Penny agreed.

"And look at all this homework," Daisy added. "I'm tired, tired, tired of homework!"

Minnie saw a man lying in a hammock reading a book.
"That man sure is lucky!" she said. "I wish I had time to read all my favorite storybooks! If I were a grown-up, I'd read whatever I wanted — whenever I wanted to!"

As the girls passed the park, they saw some people playing tennis.

"Well, if I were a grown-up," Penny said, "I'd play tennis all day, and stay up as late as I wanted to, and watch all the sports shows on TV!"

"I'd eat all the ice cream I wanted," Clarabelle sighed as an ice-cream truck jingled its bell nearby. She felt in her pockets for money to buy a cone, but all she found was a squished jelly bean.

Down the street, in front of Mrs. Baxter's house, the girls saw a pretty lady get off a bus with her arms full of pink and white shopping bags. "Wow!" Daisy said. "If I were a grown-up, I'd go shopping every day!" "And have lots of money to spend, too!" Clarabelle added.

"Grown-ups have more fun," Penny said. "I wish I were older already."

Mrs. Baxter was raking her yard as the girls stood there chatting. "I couldn't help overhearing you," she said. "You're just the girls I need! I'll be out of town all day tomorrow, and I could sure use some housesitters. I'll pay you to do my chores and to take care of my parrot. You can fix whatever you want for lunch and dinner, and stay up until I get back — but you have to get permission first. How does that sound?"

"WOW!" Minnie shouted. "A real job!"

"And a chance to eat whatever we want to eat," Clarabelle grinned.

"And to stay up late," Penny added.

"And to earn money to go shopping!" Daisy said, smiling.

"We'll be just like grown-ups!" they shouted as they ran home to ask for permission.

Bright and early the next day, Minnie, Clarabelle, Penny, and Daisy arrived at Mrs. Baxter's house.

"The list of chores is on the kitchen table," she told them as she walked to her car. "Help yourself to anything you want to eat! I'll be back late tonight!"

"'Bye, Mrs. Baxter," the girls called from the doorway. "We'll take good care of everything for you!"

"Okay, let's get started!" Daisy yelled as they ran into the kitchen to read Mrs. Baxter's list of chores.

"Gosh," Penny said when she saw the list, "there's a lot to do!"

"We'll all help," Minnie said. "And just think, we're on our own all day! This is going to be fun!"

Minnie put on one of Mrs. Baxter's aprons. It flopped down to her ankles. "I even look like a grown-up," she giggled.

"We'll wash the dishes," Minnie said. She and Penny filled the sink with soapy bubbles.

"I know a great way to mop floors," Daisy said. "With my feet!" Everyone laughed as she took off her shoes and slid across the floor in her socks.

"Well, watch me!" giggled Clarabelle as she balanced a wastebasket on her head.

Next, it was time to feed Ruffles, Mrs. Baxter's parrot. But when Minnie opened the birdcage, the parrot flew out!

"Quick, help me catch Ruffles!" Minnie yelled.

The girls chased Ruffles through the kitchen and the living room, around the bedroom, and into the den. Finally, he landed on the TV. Minnie cupped her hands gently over the bird. She put him back in his cage and shut the door tight.

"Ruffles, you wore me out!" Minnie laughed. "I need to rest."

"Well, I'm ready for lunch!" Clarabelle said. "I'm starving."

Soon Daisy, Minnie, and Penny were enjoying peanut butter sandwiches and sipping apple juice. But Clarabelle ate a triple-scoop ice-cream sundae with oodles of chocolate sauce, bananas, and marshmallows.

"That's not a very healthy lunch," Minnie said.

"But when you're a grown-up, you can eat whatever you want to — and besides, this is yummy!" Clarabelle told her.

After lunch, no one felt like going back to work. Penny turned on the TV. "A tennis match!" she shouted. "I want to see this!"

"Let's look at Mrs. Baxter's collection," Daisy said to Clarabelle. She pointed to a row of dolls and animals on the shelf.

Minnie saw a book with beautiful pictures in it lying open on the coffee table. She started to read it, but then she remembered the list of chores.

"Come on, everybody," Minnie said to her friends. "We still have work to do."

"Minnie, we're tired," everyone groaned, but they followed her outside to finish their chores.

All afternoon, they worked in the yard. Minnie and Penny swept the porch and sidewalk while Daisy watered the flower beds. But there was no time to play and spray each other with the hose. Clarabelle raked up piles of old brown leaves. But there was no time to jump in them.

"There, we're done!" Minnie said at last. "Now it's time to fix dinner! And we can stay up late to watch TV after we eat!"

"I'm too tired to move!" Daisy said as they went inside.

"Food — ugh," Clarabelle groaned. "My tummy hurts. I think it was all that chocolate sauce."

"Why don't you lie down on the sofa, Clarabelle," Minnie suggested. "We'll fix dinner and you can eat later if you feel better."

"That's a good idea, Minnie," Clarabelle said. She turned on the TV and lay down on the couch to watch.

"Look, here's a frozen pizza," Minnie said. She put the pizza on a baking sheet and slid it into the oven.

Daisy found a bakery box and peeked inside. "Yum, chocolate cupcakes — my favorite!" she said. "I'm going to eat one right now!"

Penny set the table. "I'm going to watch TV while the pizza cooks," she said. "It's almost time for my favorite show — 'Sports Galore!'"

"Come and get it," Minnie called to her friends when the pizza was ready. But no one answered. Minnie looked around. Penny and Clarabelle were fast asleep on the couch. And Daisy was asleep at the table — with her head on the bakery box!

I guess I'll have to eat this pizza by myself, Minnie thought. She picked up a slice, but suddenly she felt too tired to chew! *I'll just rest my eyes a minute,* she told herself. Minnie closed her eyes — and soon she was sound asleep, too!

The next thing Minnie knew, Mrs. Baxter was gently tapping her shoulder. "Wake up, Minnie! It's time to go home," she called softly.

Minnie rubbed her eyes. Daisy and Clarabelle were blinking and yawning, too. Outside it was very dark.

"Thank you, girls, for taking care of everything while I was gone," Mrs. Baxter said. "Here's your money for a job well done. Now I'll drive you home."

They all piled into Mrs. Baxter's car.

"Did you have a good day?" she asked.

"Yes, thank you," they answered sleepily.

"But I'm ready for bed," yawned Penny. "Staying up late like grown-ups makes me tired!"

"I didn't know grown-ups worked so hard!" Daisy agreed. "School doesn't seem so bad after all!"

"I really learned something today!" Minnie smiled sleepily as Mrs. Baxter stopped in front of her house. "I'm glad I'm not a grown-up yet. Being a kid is just fine for now!"